POKéMON
The First Movie

MEWTWO
STRIKES BACK ™

Adapted by Justine & Ron Fontes

A GOLDEN BOOK® • NEW YORK
Golden Books Publishing Company, Inc.
New York, New York 10106

We'd be happy to answer your questions and hear your comments.
Please call us toll free at 1-888-READ-2-ME (1-888-732-3263).
Hours: 8 AM—8 PM EST, weekdays. US and Canada only.

In a laboratory on far-off New Island, the most powerful Pokémon of all was born.

"Who am I? What am I? Where am I?" the newborn Pokémon asked the scientists hovering outside its tank.

"For ten years we have struggled to create a superclone of the great, rare Mew. You are Mewtwo—with awesome psychic powers," one scientist explained.

Mewtwo raged. "I am not just an experiment!"

The powerful Pokémon was so angry, it destroyed the lab!

The Boss arrived as flames engulfed New Island. He told Mewtwo, "You are more than an experiment. You will be my partner. With your psychic powers, we can rule the world!"

But Mewtwo did not wish to work for the evil Boss. The newest Pokémon decided to find its own reason for living.

Not long after, Ash, Brock, Misty, Pikachu, and Togepi were enjoying a picnic when a Dragonite delivered a mysterious invitation. A hologram of a young woman appeared and she said, "My Master, the greatest Pokémon trainer, invites you to his palace on New Island. A ferry will leave from Old Shore Wharf this afternoon."

Ash and his friends crossed the stormy sea to New Island. There, the young woman took them to a great hall already filled with other Pokémon trainers. She said, "The time has come for your encounter with the greatest Pokémon Master on Earth!"

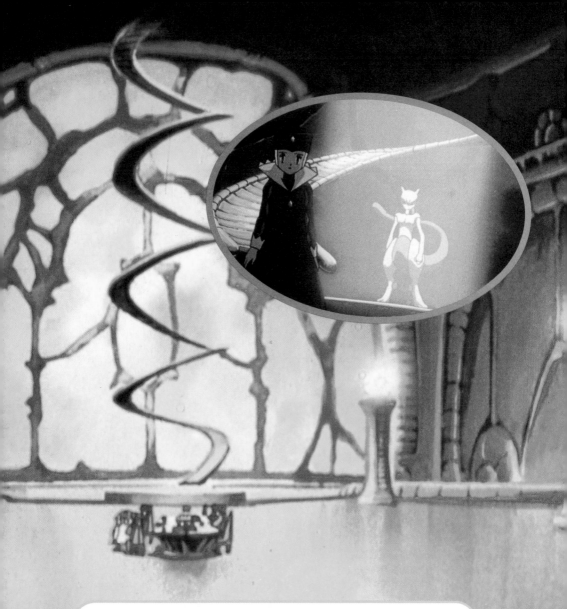

Mewtwo entered and everyone gasped! The young woman continued, "This is the Master of New Island, and soon, the whole world—Mewtwo!"

A boy named Fergus shouted, "A Pokémon can't be a Pokémon trainer!"

Mewtwo answered with its mind, not its mouth. Everyone heard the psychic Pokémon's angry mental voice, "Who are you to object, human? I make my own rules!"

Then, using only the awesome powers of its mind, Mewtwo flung Fergus far across the room!

And while the human trainers and their Pokémon reeled in shock, Mewtwo used its powers to call the other Pokémon clones being held in laboratory tanks. Mewtwo hated humans for treating it like a slave of science, and it couldn't forgive its fellow Pokémon for serving mankind.

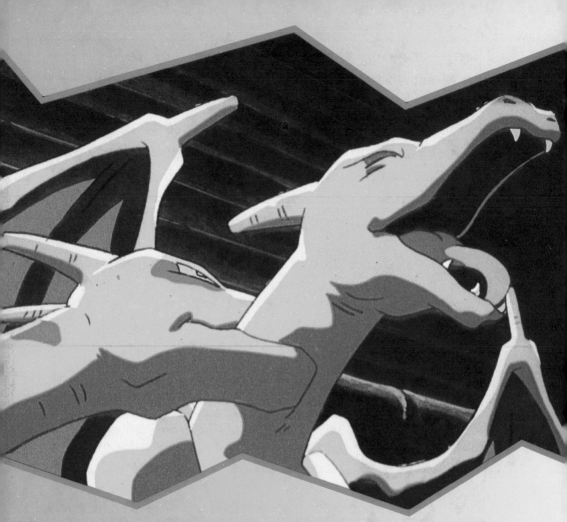

A battle began between the trainers and their loyal Pokémon, and Mewtwo with its army of clones. Even the bravest Pokémon could not beat the look-alike clones.

Mewtwo savored its victory. "I now claim my prize—your Pokémon! I will make clones of them to join my army. We will be safe on this island while my storm destroys the planet!"

He threw black Poké Balls to capture the trainer's Pokémon.

Brave little Pikachu ran as fast as it could!
"Keep running, Pikachu!" Ash called.
But the little Pokémon fell—down, down
toward the cloning machine! Ash dove after
Pikachu and saved it from the machine.
But who would save Ash from Mewtwo?
Suddenly, Mew appeared!

"I will now prove that Mewtwo is superior to Mew!" Mewtwo declared.

Meowth interpreted Mew's reply, "Mew says ya don't prove anythin' by showin' off a lot o' special powers; a Pokémon's real strength comes from the heart."

The battle raged. It was Pokémon against clone. Only Pikachu refused to fight— even when its evil clone kept hitting it.

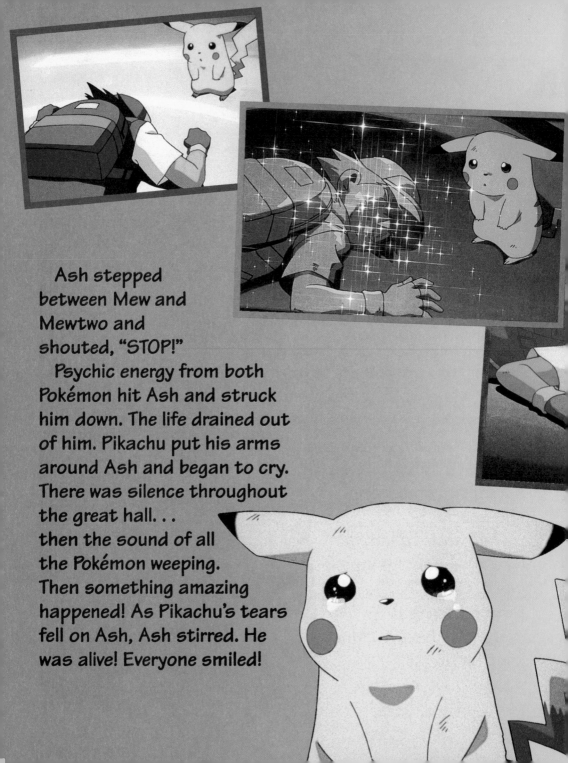

Ash stepped between Mew and Mewtwo and shouted, "STOP!"

Psychic energy from both Pokémon hit Ash and struck him down. The life drained out of him. Pikachu put his arms around Ash and began to cry. There was silence throughout the great hall. . . then the sound of all the Pokémon weeping. Then something amazing happened! As Pikachu's tears fell on Ash, Ash stirred. He was alive! Everyone smiled!

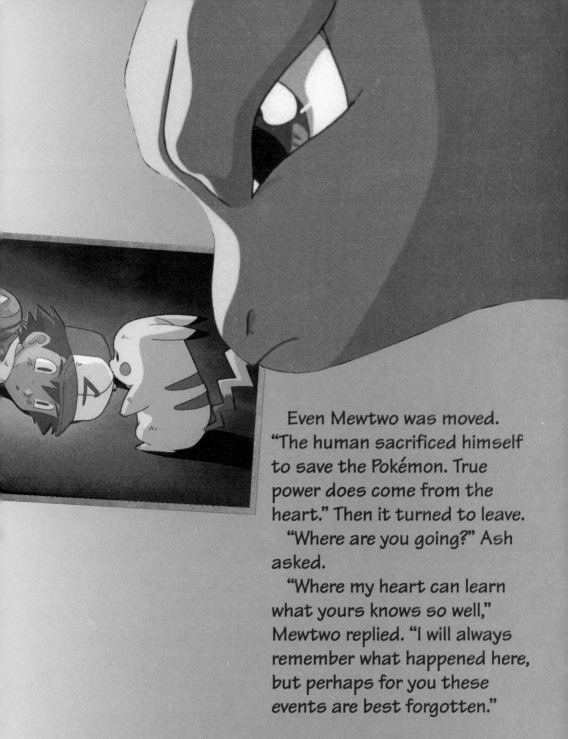

Even Mewtwo was moved. "The human sacrificed himself to save the Pokémon. True power does come from the heart." Then it turned to leave.

"Where are you going?" Ash asked.

"Where my heart can learn what yours knows so well," Mewtwo replied. "I will always remember what happened here, but perhaps for you these events are best forgotten."

With that, Mewtwo turned back time, so Ash and his friends found themselves at Old Shore Wharf wondering why the ferry to New Island had been cancelled. And so ended the greatest Pokémon adventure that never was!